ALEXANDER'S Pretending Day

by **BUNNY CRUMPACKER**   illustrated by **DAN ANDREASEN**

Dutton Children's Books · New York

For Casey, who always asked the best questions
—B.C.

For little Katrina
—D.A.

Text copyright © 2005 by Bunny Crumpacker
Illustrations copyright © 2005 by Dan Andreasen

Library of Congress Cataloging-in-Publication Data
Crumpacker, Bunny.
Alexander's pretending day / by Bunny Crumpacker; illustrated by Dan Andreasen.—1st ed. p. cm.
Summary: When Alexander asks his mother questions, they use their imaginations to play together.
ISBN 0-525-46936-2
[1. Mother and child—Fiction. 2. Imagination—Fiction.] I. Andreasen, Dan, ill. II. Title.
PZ7.C88753A1 2005
[E]—dc22 2004012094

Published in the United States by Dutton Children's Books,
a division of Penguin Young Readers Group
345 Hudson Street, New York, New York 10014
www.penguin.com

Designed by Gloria Cheng

Manufactured in China · First Edition
1 3 5 7 9 10 8 6 4 2

Alexander was sitting at the table with his mother and drawing pictures with his new birthday crayons. It was a quiet morning and a good time for pretending.

"Pretend I'm a mouse," Alexander said to his mother. "Pretend I'm a really hungry mouse."

"And I'm sitting on the floor right in front of you and saying,
'Squeak, squeak, squeak!' What would you do?"

Alexander's mother put her newspaper down and looked at him.

"I'd give you a delicious piece of cheese," she said. "What would you do if I did that?"

"I'd say 'Squeak, squeak,'" Alexander said. "That means 'Thank you.'"

"You're welcome," Alexander's mother said.

"But I'd really like a piece of cheese," Alexander said. "Please?"

Alexander's mother gave him a piece of cheese and a cracker and a glass of juice.

"Squeak, squeak," Alexander said.

"You're welcome," his mother said, and she picked up her newspaper again and started to read.

"But what if I turned into an angry lion," Alexander said before she could turn the page. "And I roared at you." He roared, his mouth open wide. "What would you do if I did that?"

His mother thought for a minute.

"I wouldn't roar back," she said. "Lions can roar louder than I can. I think I'd just ask you very politely if you'd like to have your ears scratched or your tummy tickled."

"I'd say yes," Alexander said. "I always like to have my tummy tickled—if I can say when to stop."

"Lions can always say when to stop," his mother said.

"Now pretend I'm a train," Alexander said. "I come rolling down the railroad track, and I'm puffing smoke and blowing my whistle really loud, and I don't even stop to say hello. What would you do?"

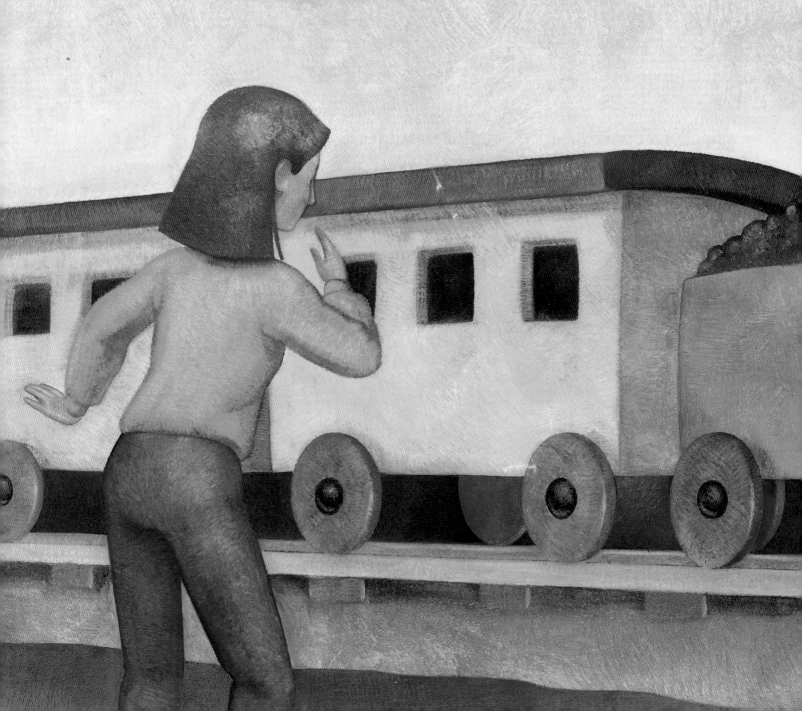

"I'd wait at the crossing," his mother said. "I'd count your cars as you went by, and I'd wave at your caboose. Then I'd rush right home so I could be waiting for you when you got there."

"What if I got there and I was a monster—a big, mean monster—and I came knocking at your door. What would you do?"

"I'd pretend I wasn't home," his mother said.

"You couldn't do that!" Alexander answered. "It's nighttime and the lights are on. I'd know you were home."

"Well, then," his mother said, "I guess I'd have to ask you to come in. I'd see if you wanted any cookies or tea. I'd find out what kind of sandwich was your favorite and I'd make it for you, and we'd get to be friends. I wouldn't mind having a monster for a friend."

"That sounds good," Alexander said. "The sandwich should be cream cheese and honey, and you can have my tea."

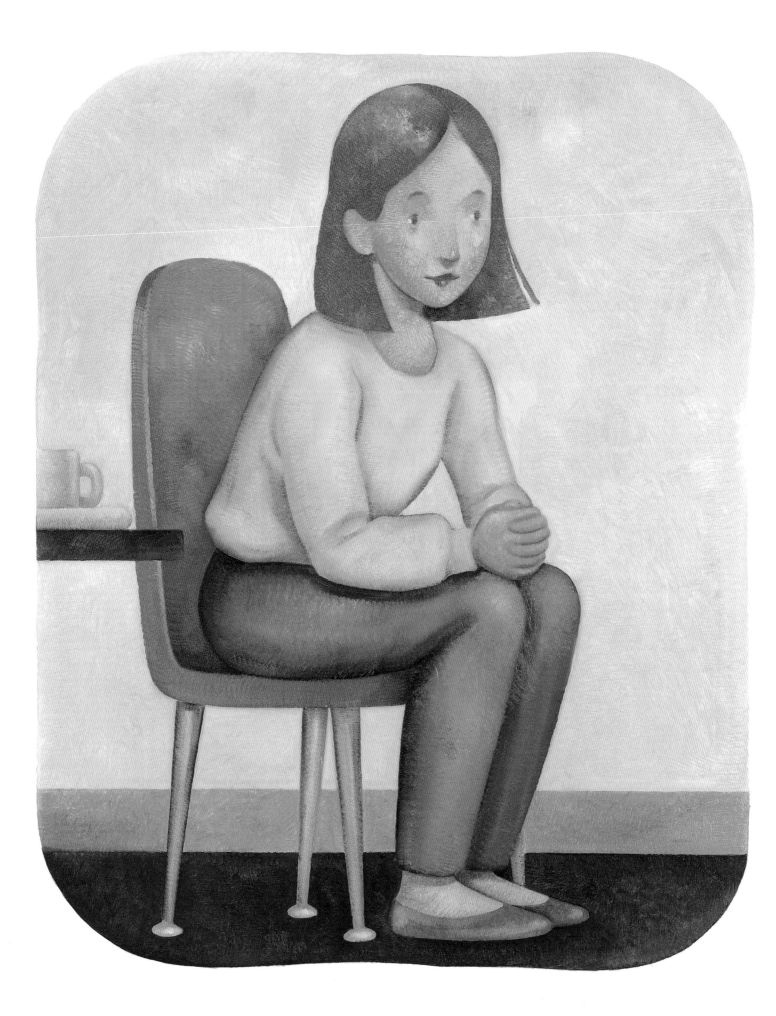

"What if I ran away like a deep, strong river," Alexander asked, "and I went so fast you couldn't catch me. What would you do?"

"I'd find a bridge," Alexander's mother said. "I'd walk across it, from one side of you to the other. Maybe I'd drop a leaf over the side and watch you play with it as it floated away. And then I'd find a sandy shore, and I'd stick my toes in the water."

"I'd tickle your toes," Alexander said.

"Then I'd laugh," Alexander's mother said.

But she tickled him instead.

"No more tickling. I'm a dinosaur now, stomping all over and looking in all the windows. What would you do?"

"What I'd like to do," his mother said, "is have a ride on your back. I'd be able to see really far from up there." She thought for a minute. "Are you a friendly dinosaur?"

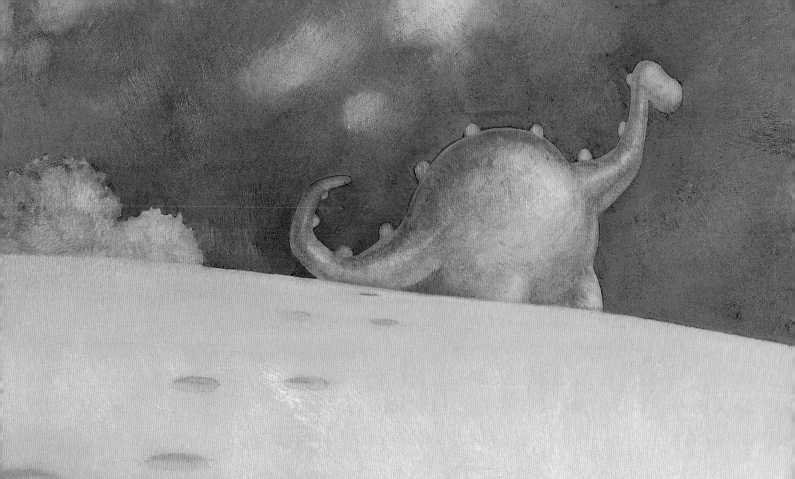

"I'm NOT a friendly dinosaur," Alexander growled. "I'm a GROUCHY dinosaur."

"That rules out the ride," Alexander's mother said. "I guess I would just have to wait for you to leave. And I'd save your footprints, so I could show them to you when you were just you again."

"Hardly anybody has dinosaur footprints," Alexander said.

"That's true," said his mother.

"Pretend I'm a book," Alexander said, "hiding in the library on a shelf with a lot of other books that look just the same. How would you find me?"

"I'd look you up under *Alexander*," his mother said, "and you'd be right at the beginning, because *Alexander* begins with *A*. I'd sit down and read you from cover to cover."

"I'd be a good story," Alexander said. "It would be about how I lived with a family of penguins. I'd swim underwater and make funny noises, and my feet would never be cold."

"You'd have to eat raw fish," his mother said.

Alexander thought. "It's just a story," he said.

"It's a good story," his mother said. "I like it."

"What if you didn't have a boy like me?" Alexander asked. "What would you do?"

"I would want a boy like you very much," his mother said. "I think I'd be sad until I had one, and then I would be very, very happy."

"Like now?" Alexander asked.

"Yes," said his mother, "like now."